CLAUDIA CRISTINA CORTEZ

UNCOMPLICATES YOUR LIFE

Advice

ABOUT WORK AND PLAY

BY DIANA G. GALLAGHER

ILLUSTRATED BY BRANN GARVEY

STONE ARCH BOOKS
a capstone imprint

Claudia Cristina Cortez are published by Stone Arch Books
A Capstone Imprint
151 Good Counsel Drive, P.O. Box 669
Mankato, Minnesota 56002
www.capstonepub.com

Printed in the United States of America in Stevens Point, Wisconsin.
092009
005619WZS10

Library of Congress Cataloging-in-Publication Data
Gallagher, Diana G.
    Advice about work and play: Claudia Cristina Cortez uncomplicates your life /
    by Diana G. Gallagher; illustrated by Brann Garvey.
    p. cm. — (Claudia Cristina Cortez)
    ISBN 978-1-4342-1908-4 (library binding)
    ISBN 978-1-4342-2253-4 (pbk.)
    1. Teenagers—Vocational guidance—Juvenile literature. 2. Part-time
employment—Juvenile literature. 3. Leisure—Juvenile literature. I. Garvey, Brann.
II. Title.
    HF5381.2.G35 2010
    331.702083'5—dc22   2009036135

ART DIRECTOR/GRAPHIC DESIGNER: *Kay Fraser*
PRODUCTION SPECIALIST: *Michelle Biedscheid*
PHOTO CREDITS: *Delaney Photography*

CLAUDIA

CAST OF

CLAUDIA
That's me. I'm thirteen, and I'm in the seventh grade at Pine Tree Middle School. I live with my mom, my dad, and my brother, Jimmy. I have one cat, Ping-Ping. I like music, baseball, and hanging out with my friends.

MONICA is my very best friend. We met when we were really little, and we've been best friends ever since. I don't know what I'd do without her! Monica loves horses. In fact, when she grows up, she wants to be an Olympic rider!

MONICA

BECCA is one of my closest friends. She lives next door to Monica. Becca is really, really smart. She gets good grades. She's also really good at art.

BECCA

CHARACTERS

TOMMY's our class clown. Sometimes he's really funny, but sometimes he is just annoying. Becca has a crush on him . . . but I'd never tell.

TOMMY

PETER

I think **PETER** is probably the smartest person I've ever met. Seriously. He's even smarter than our teachers! He's also one of my friends. Which is lucky, because sometimes he helps me with homework.

ADAM and I met when we were in third grade. Now that we're teenagers, we don't spend as much time together as we did when we were kids, but he's always there for me when I need him. (Plus, he's the only person who wants to talk about baseball with me!)

ADAM

CAST OF

JIMMY is my big brother. He's obsessed with video games and computers. He doesn't talk to me very much, except when I do something to annoy him. I usually try to stay out of his way, but sometimes he helps me out.

JIMMY

NICK is my annoying seven-year-old neighbor. I get stuck babysitting him a lot. He likes to make me miserable. (Okay, he's not that bad ALL of the time . . . just most of the time.)

NICK

MRS. WRIGHT is Nick's mom. Sometimes she pays me to babysit Nick, but sometimes she doesn't. Mom says that we should help our neighbors out without expecting something in return. But it is still a bummer.

MS. WRIGHT

CHARACTERS

Every school has a bully, and **JENNY** is ours. She's the tallest person in our class, and the meanest, too. She always threatens to stomp people. No one's ever seen her stomp anyone, but that doesn't mean it hasn't happened!

ANNA is the most popular girl at our school. Everyone wants to be friends with her. I think that's weird, because Anna can be really, really mean. I mostly try to stay away from her.

MR. AND MRS. GOMEZ are my neighbors. Even though they are old enough to be my grandparents, I consider them my good friends. They taught me some great old dances, and they help me earn money by paying me to help in the yard and walk their dog, Fancy.

INTRODUCTION

Grown-ups don't understand that being a teenager is hard. My life gets more complicated every day! I have to balance school, work, friends, and family. **I'M REALLY BUSY!** School takes up most of my time. But I also want to hang out with my friends. My family expects me to spend time with them. And I need to find time to earn some money. It's not easy.

My mom says I should enjoy not having any responsibilities. I think she's **CRAZY!** I have **tons** of responsibilities. I'm responsible for being a good student. I'm responsible for being a good daughter and sister. I'm responsible for being a good friend. And I'm responsible for earning spending money. How else can I buy the things my parents say I don't need?

On the other hand, I do get to spend a lot of time having **FUN**. This book is about those two things: *earning money* and **having fun**. And I know a lot about both of them!

▷ CHAPTER 1
GET TO WORK:
The right job for you

My mom likes to say that being in school is my job. And it's true, I spend A LOT of time every week at school. It's almost as much time as my dad spends at his job at the computer store. But nobody pays me for going to school. And my parents don't give me an allowance. So I need to make money somehow.

When you're little, you **NEVER** have to worry about money. Nobody ever expects you to pay for things. And your parents buy you the things you need.

That all changes when you become a teenager. Now that I'm thirteen, my parents expect me to have my own money. I **need** money to go out with my friends. I use it to buy DVDs and magazines and pay for movies. And I save it for the big stuff, like a car and my college fund.

Some thirteen-year-olds are lucky. Their parents pay for EVERYTHING. I'm not one of them! I have to work for the things I need. I don't mind working. If I didn't like the jobs I do, I wouldn't do them. I would find a job I did like to do. The work itself isn't the hard part.

The hard part is:

1. **Finding customers**

2. **Keeping customers happy**

3. **Saving money**

I think I've done a pretty good job of taking care of all three of the things on that list. Now I have so many customers that sometimes I actually have to say NO to a job! I'm saving lots of money, although I don't have enough for that car yet. But I think I might be able to earn enough in the next three years. As long as it's not a very expensive car.

Working is fun. It's a great way to meet your neighbors, get exercise, and help other people. And make money, of course!

I turned some of my *favorite hobbies* into **money-making opportunities**. I like dogs, so I became a dog walker. I like kids, so I became a babysitter.

The problem is, when you're thirteen, you can't work at a R**EAL** job (like my brother, who works at our dad's computer store). Our options are limited. But there are ways to find work you can do.

Start by talking to your parents. They might pay you to do jobs around the house. Or they might know of friends or neighbors who could use your help.

You can also talk to your friends about jobs they do.

Common jobs for thirteen-year-olds are:

- babysitter
- gardening helper
- snow shoveler
- dog walker
- lawn mower
- newspaper delivery person

FIND THE PERFECT JOB

To find your perfect job, you'll need to think about a few things. *Ask yourself the following questions:*

1. WHAT ARE MY HOBBIES AND INTERESTS? Do you have any hobbies that could turn into jobs?

2. WHAT ARE OTHER THINGS I'M GOOD AT? If you are good with animals, maybe you'd make a good dog walker or pet sitter.

3. HOW MUCH MONEY DO I WANT TO MAKE? Do you need a job that pays a lot? Or are you willing to work more?

4. HOW MUCH TIME AM I WILLING TO SPEND WORKING? Do you need one customer, or many?

5. WHO WILL BE MY CUSTOMERS? What kind of people need your help and will pay you?

6. HOW WILL I STILL HAVE TIME FOR SCHOOL, FAMILY, AND FRIENDS? What kind of schedule will you have?

1. If you could create the **PERFECT DAY**, it would be:

a. Dark and rainy — perfect for watching **movies**

b. Warm and sunny — perfect for being outside

c. Cool and windy — perfect for taking long **walks**

d. It doesn't matter, but no snow!

2. Which of these statements is *most true* about you?

a. I love little kids.

b. I don't mind getting **DIRTY**.

c. I'm an animal lover.

d. I like *helping* people.

3. When you were a kid, what was your *favorite* way to spend your time?

a. Watching DVDs and playing hide-and-seek

b. Being **outside**, no matter what you were doing

c. Playing with your family dog or visiting the zoo

d. Spending time with your **grandparents**

4. What's your *style?*

a. I'm a **mix**, sometimes crazy, sometimes calm.

b. I'm a **HARD WORKER**. I work till the job's done.

c. I'm **calm but firm**. I'm not bossy, but I'm good at getting things done my way.

d. I'm a **GREAT** listener.

If you chose:

MOSTLY A'S: You'd be a great babysitter! Check out page 16 for more.

MOSTLY B'S: Lawn mowing or gardening is the perfect job for you. See pages 20 and 22.

MOSTLY C'S: All the dogs in town will be glad you started taking them for walks. Turn to page 18.

MOSTLY D'S: Consider running errands for neighbors! Flip to page 26 for more information.

I love kids. Well, most kids, anyway. I don't love my BRATTY seven-year-old neighbor, Nick Wright. But I do love most kids. So it's pretty obvious that I love babysitting.

I don't like everything about babysitting. Diapers are GROSS. And I really hate having to put kids to bed, because sometimes they cry about it. But I love playing with kids. It's like a chance to be a little kid again, instead of a teenager with real **problems!**

My babysitting career started with Nick. Then his mom recommended me to some of her friends. Now, I've babysat for kids of all ages — even a little baby.

I'm a good babysitter because I'm patient, I like kids, and I like playing. I have lots of ENERGY. If I was the kind of person who wasn't crazy about little kids and didn't feel like being responsible for others, I wouldn't be a very good babysitter at all.

Tips: **1.** Don't take it personally if a kid cries when his or her parents leave. That's normal, and it doesn't mean he or she doesn't like you. **2.** Be specific with parents about what they expect. Do they want you to clean? Put kids to bed? **3.** Find out about rules, like TV-watching and computer time, before the parents leave. **4.** Even if they don't ask you to, pick up the house — that's something parents love.

Pay: I get paid by the hour, and per kid. I give a discount if there's more than one kid at a time ($10 per hour for one kid, but $15 per hour for two).

What you need: Just yourself! Bring some color books or some of your old toys to be extra fun.

Be green: Don't make microwave meals. Instead, make sandwiches. Add fruit and veggies and have a picnic outside. They'll love it!

Where to find customers: Anywhere you find kids. Start with friends of your family. Let them know that if they like your babysitting skills, you'd appreciate if they'd recommend you to their friends. Soon you'll have A TON of customers.

DOGGIE DUTY

Almost every house in my neighborhood has at least one dog. My family only has a cat, Ping-ping. But since there are so many dogs in the area, it's a great place to be a dog walker.

The **Gomezes** across the street have a poodle, FANCY. I started my dog-walking career by walking Fancy once in a while. I also cleaned up her poop from their lawn. It wasn't a *glamorous* job, but I needed the money!

Then other people in the neighborhood started noticing that I was walking Fancy. Soon I had more and more clients.

I like walking dogs because, well, I like dogs! I also like being outside and getting exercise. I don't like it when I have to walk dogs in the RAIN. But I've been lucky. It hasn't rained much while I'm on dog-walking duty.

If I didn't like animals, going for walks, or being outside, I would probably **hate** being a dog walker.

Tips: **1.** Bring along treats. But make sure it's okay with the owner. Some dogs have allergies. **2.** Never walk more than two dogs at a time. It's too hard for the dogs to pay attention. **3.** If you have a problem with a dog, make sure to tell its owner. **4.** Try not to let the dog pee on anyone's lawn. Keep them near the curb. **5.** If you walk past other dogs or any little kids, keep the dog close to you. Even the nicest dog in the world gets spooked sometimes. It's safer for everyone if the dog doesn't get too close to kids.

Pay: I charge per walk, per dog. I walk some dogs every day, and some once or twice a week.

What you need: Good shoes, treats, poop bags

Be green: Use biodegradable bags to clean up dog poop. Unlike regular plastic bags, these special bags will break down in landfills.

Where to find customers: Near your house. If you have a pet, you can advertise at your veterinarian's office. And animal shelters often need volunteers to walk their dogs. You won't get paid, but you'll get lots of **doggy kisses**.

I don't mow the lawn at my house. My brother **Jimmy** does. Once a neighbor came over and told my dad our yard looked nice. He was really impressed when my dad said Jimmy mowed the lawn. He hired Jimmy on the spot!

Then that customer told one of his friends about Jimmy. That friend told another friend. Now, Jimmy has LOTS of customers — usually around ten every summer. He mows five lawns one week and five the next. It makes his Saturdays pretty busy, but he says it's worth it.

Jimmy likes mowing the lawn. He gets exercise from pushing the mower. He spends a lot of time outside. **AND HE MAKES GOOD MONEY**. He also gets to talk to a lot of our neighbors. If he didn't like being outside and being friendly to our neighbors, my brother probably wouldn't like his job mowing half the lawns in the neighborhood.

Tips: **1.** Don't forget sunscreen, a bottle of water, and your MP3 player. Mowing lawns gets loud though. So you might want to wear earplugs instead of listening to music. **2.** Wear old clothes and shoes that can get stained. **3.** You should sign a contract with your customers. Also, make sure to tell them if you're going on vacation.

Pay: Jimmy mows his customers' lawns once every two weeks. Most of them pay him once a month.

What you need: You probably don't need much, usually just old clothes and shoes. Most people will let you use their mower (unless you want to bring your own).

Be green: If you can, use a push reel mower instead of a gas mower. It takes a little longer, but it is much better for the environment.

Where to find customers: In your neighborhood, especially older people or very busy people. Look for families with a lot of little kids. Don't bother at houses that have teenage boys. One of them is probably responsible for mowing the lawn already.

I **LOVE** being outside in my mom's garden. I love being surrounded by the smell of flowers. I love feeling the sun on my skin. I even love hearing bees *buzzing* around my head. So one of my perfect jobs is helping neighbors with their gardens.

In the springtime, I help plant. Before it's warm out, I help my neighbor **Mrs. Pike** in her shed. We plant seeds in small pots of dirt. Once it's warm enough, we plant them in the ground outside. During the summer, I help weed the flower garden and the vegetable garden. When vegetables start to grow, I help gather them. And in the fall, we work together to clean up the garden and get it ready for winter.

Gardening is a great job for me. I love being outside, and I don't care if I get *MUD* under my fingernails. It probably wouldn't be a good job for someone who didn't like being outside or was worried about getting dirty.

Tips: **1.** Wear lots of sunscreen! Even if it's not sunny outside, your skin can still be damaged by the sun. Make sure to reapply the sunscreen if you're sweating a lot. **2.** Don't wear perfume or makeup, because the sweet smells will attract bees and other bugs. **3.** If you're not sure whether something is a weed, make sure to ask. You don't want to accidentally pull out a beautiful flower! **4.** Drink lots of water when you're outside so that you don't overheat.

Pay: Mrs. Pike pays me by the hour.

Be green: Don't use chemicals to kill weeds or bugs.

What you need: I have a few sets of clothes that can get dirty. I keep them in a plastic bag and wash them separately from my other clothes. I also wear a baseball cap. It helps keep my head and face from getting sunburned. You'll also need a water bottle and sunscreen. Gardening gloves and tools (a spade, a small bucket) can help, but they aren't necessary.

Where to find customers: In your neighborhood or nearby, so that you can walk or bike there.

SCOOP THAT SNOW

Lawn-mowing season is over in the winter. But Jimmy stays busy. He shovels snow out of people's driveways and sidewalks. *And he makes a lot of money!*

Jimmy is perfect for the job because he loves being outside. (Even when it's really cold out.) He doesn't mind getting up early, at least when he has a job to do. He's **dependable**, so his clients know they can count on him. And he likes the exercise he gets from shoveling heavy piles of snow.

Jimmy sets up his customers at the beginning of the winter. This year, he has five families. If he had more, it would take too long to shovel all the snow. Then his customers wouldn't be happy. He sets up a contract with each family. The contract says what areas Jimmy will shovel and how much he'll be paid.

Every time it snows, Jimmy's phone starts ringing. Once the snow stops, he heads out to each of the five houses. He usually needs a break between each house. **SHOVELING SNOW IS REALLY HARD WORK!**

Tips: **1.** If you have more than one customer, take a break between houses. **2.** Don't forget to let your customers know when you'll be out of town. If it snows while you're gone, they'll have to either find another snow-shoveler or do it themselves. **3.** Dress in layers. Shoveling snow can work up a sweat!

Pay: Jimmy usually charges per snowfall. Every time he shovels someone's sidewalk, he gets paid. But he does have a special agreement with one of his customers. **Mrs. Grove** offered him **$200** for the whole winter. She paid half on December 1 and half on April 15. Anytime it snowed between those two dates, Jimmy knew he was responsible for shoveling.

What you need: Some customers have their own shovels, but it helps if you have a good one that you like. It should be lightweight and shaped to move lots of snow. You also need warm clothes, a hat, and waterproof gloves.

Be green: Use a shovel, not a snowblower.

Where to find customers: In your neighborhood. You don't want to have to travel any farther than a few blocks to shovel snow.

Let's say you hate shopping. You don't like helping other people. And you would rather do a million push-ups than stand in long lines. Then this isn't the job for you. But if you are *trustworthy*, DEPENDABLE, and **love shopping**, you'll probably be great at this.

Lots of older people, people who are very busy, and parents of small children need help getting everyday errands done. That's where you come in.

HERE'S HOW IT WORKS. You show up at your customer's house. They give you a list of things they need and the money to pay for the items. Then you head out to the store. After picking up everything on the list, you bring it back to their house. Then they pay you.

This is a hard job to get because the customer needs to be able to **TRUST YOU.** They have to be sure that you're not going to just take off with their money. They also have to be sure that you'll do a good job: that you'll get the 1% milk instead of whole, the green grapes instead of red, the right brand of peanut butter.

Tips: **1.** Ask your questions before you go shopping. If you're not sure what an item is, ask. Be specific about whether you should buy brand names or generic items. Ask what you should do if the cost is more than expected. **2.** A customer may be concerned about giving you money to pay for their items. You could suggest that they buy a gift card to the store. You can use that to pay for their purchases.

Pay: Charge by the trip or by the number of stores you have to visit.

You'll need: You don't need much for this job. A notebook could come in handy, so you can take notes on each of your customers. You might also want a bike to make getting from place to place easier.

Be green: Bring a reusable canvas bag to carry home groceries. The earth will thank you, and so will your customers!

Where to find customers: Start with people you know, people who trust you. Try friends of your family or people you know from church or school.

My friend **ADAM** delivers newspapers to make money.

Every Saturday morning, Adam gets up early. The papers were delivered to his house on Friday night, so he's ready to go as soon as he gets dressed.

He and his dad get on their bikes. Then they ride around the neighborhood and drop off newspapers at the houses of everyone who gets the *Harmon County Herald.*

Adam loves being outside, and he loves riding his bike. So does his dad. Adam wanted a job that didn't involve a lot of talking to people. (He can be kind of shy.) If he really liked talking to people, this wouldn't be the best job for him.

He also doesn't mind being outside when it's cold or rainy. If he only wanted to go outside when it was sunny and warm, he wouldn't make a very good newspaper carrier!

Tips: **1.** Don't throw the newspaper into a puddle. Try to get it as close to the person's front door as possible. They'll appreciate not having to walk far to get their paper. **2.** Wear cool clothes in the summer and warm clothes in the winter. **3.** Until you get to know your route, bring an adult with you just to be on the safe side.

Pay: The newspaper delivery company pays you, usually weekly.

You need: Not much. A bike, or a parent to drive you. If you ride a bike, you'll need a sturdy bag to hold the newspapers.

Be green: Instead of asking your parents to drive you to each house, ride your bike or walk. Your mom or dad can ride or walk along with you. It is better for your body and better for the environment.

Where to find customers: Newspapers usually advertise that they're looking for paper carriers in the classified section. Unlike the old days, you won't be responsible for making sure people pay or for finding new subscribers.

▷ CHAPTER 2
WHO NEEDS YOU?
Finding customers

You want to make money. What do you do first? **Find people who will pay you to do something.**

But it's not that easy.

Some people don't want to pay a teenager to do things. You have to prove to them that you're responsible.

You're also competing with other people who want the same job. So you'll have to prove you're the best person to hire.

But the hardest part isn't proving you're responsible. It isn't proving you're the best person for the job. The hardest part is letting people know that you're available, that you EXIST!

You need to get your name out there. You need to let people know you're looking for customers. And you need to sound professional, responsible, and worth the money.

Here are a few ways to get customers.

1. NETWORKING

Networking means going out and meeting people.
Go to neighborhood parties. Or go door-to-door in your
neighborhood or apartment building. Tell people who
you are. Hopefully they'll remember you when they
need a job done.

2. ADVERTISING

I'm sure you know what advertising is. Commercials
during breaks on TV shows. Big billboards on the
highway. Ads in newspapers or magazines, full of
models and shiny cars. You're probably thinking,
"I CAN NEVER AFFORD THAT!" You're right. But you can
still advertise. You just have to get creative about it.

3. WORD-OF-MOUTH

Word-of-mouth means that someone tells their
friends about you. Let's say someone asks Mrs. Wright
for the name of a good babysitter. I want her to say,
"You need to hire Claudia! She's the best." You
get good word-of-mouth by being a good employee.

Follow these rules to impress the people you meet. They could be future customers.

- **DO** look good. Wear clean clothes. Make sure your hair is clean and dry. And brush your teeth. **DON'T** spend a lot of money on a new wardrobe for an interview.

- **DO** be polite. Use good manners. Thank the person for taking the time to talk to you. **DON'T** curse or use too much slang.

- **DO** smile. It shows that you're a kind, confident person (even if you're feeling really nervous). **DON'T** frown or look crabby.

- **DO** make eye contact with the person you're talking to. **DON'T** fidget or look at the ground while you're talking.

- **DO** listen carefully. If you're not sure about something, ask questions. **DON'T** feel too nervous to ask questions. Adults like it when you try to understand something fully.

- **DO** shake hands. This shows that you're mature. **DON'T** worry if you think your hands might be sweaty. As you lift up your hand, you can quickly brush it against your clothes to dry it off.

- **DO** take deep breaths and breathe slowly. That will help you feel calmer. **DON'T** worry if you feel your heart speed up. That is normal when you're under pressure. Talking to someone new is a kind of pressure. Just take more deep breaths.

- **DO** practice ahead of time. Practice makes perfect. Use a mirror to practice what you'd like to say to the person you're trying to impress. **DON'T** just wing it. Instead, be prepared.

- **DO** talk slowly. **DON'T** rush.

- **DO** your best. **DON'T** worry. You'll be great!

So you can't afford a BIG, fancy ad in the *New York Times* or a commercial during the Super Bowl. That's okay. You don't need that kind of advertisement.

You can put an ad in your school paper or local paper, though. You could create an ad that can be copied into the paper. Try making one on a computer or by hand.

A classified ad might be even better. The classifieds are **SHORT, TEXT-ONLY ADS** that run in the back of the newspaper. That's where people go looking for items to buy or sell and people to hire.

No matter what kind of ad you use, remember the more space you use, the more it will cost you. When you write your ad, decide what the most important information is. Classified ads often charge by the word. So the SHORTER your ad is, the *more money you'll save.*

Here are some examples of classified ads.

Responsible, mature

13-year-old girl seeks babysitting jobs. Have great references. Available after school and on weekends. Email ClaudiaJobs@email.com.

Friendly dog-lover

seeks dogs to walk. Available after school and on weekends. Will walk daily or weekly. Email ClaudiaJobs@email.com.

Flower power!

Looking for gardening help? Email ClaudiaJobs@ email.com. Available after school and on weekends. References available.

Need a hand?

I'll help you run errands. Email me: ClaudiaJobs@ email.com.

I can help!

Email ClaudiaJobs@email. com.

Don't spend a lot of money on advertising. It's not worth it unless you've tried other options first. After all, you're trying to MAKE money, **NOT SPEND IT!**

WOW 'EM WITH A WEBSITE

I have lots of customers now. But if I ever want more, I'll ask my computer-whiz brother to help me create a **WEBSITE.**

A website is a great way to find customers who don't live nearby. Of course, you'll need to decide if it's worth it. If you don't want to babysit on the other side of town, it might not make sense to have a website.

But a website is a good way for people to get more information about you without needing to call you or talk to others who know you. *Anyone* will be able to access your website **anytime.**

Of course, like anything else on the Internet, you need to be careful. Make sure your parents go with you to meet possible customers. *Never, ever* meet anyone from the Internet without bringing an adult with you. That's good business sense **AND** good common sense.

Information to include on your website:

- **A page about you.** Talk about your hobbies, interests, and favorite subjects in school.

- **Contact information.** Don't include your phone number. Just use an email address. Set up a special email account to use for your website (something like "claudiasjobs@emailaddress. com"). Don't put your last name or address anywhere on the site. This protects you and your family from creeps!

- **Positive comments** from your customers. Like this. (Make sure they're true!)

"CLAUDIA IS THE BEST POOP-SCOOPER I KNOW!"
-- MR. GOMEZ

"WHEN CLAUDIA BABYSITS, MY SON IS WELL TAKEN CARE OF."
-- MRS. WRIGHT

- **Jobs** you are willing to do.

- **Payment information.** Let people know how much you charge for each job.

SUPER SIGNS by Becca

I love art, so making posters is one of my *favorite* things to do. They're also a great way to advertise your services.

Follow these tips to make your poster look amazing:

USE THE COLOR BLUE. Blue is a color that makes people feel safe and protected. It is also calming. It makes people feel good. Don't make your whole poster blue. Maybe just use it for the headline.

INCLUDE AT LEAST ONE IMAGE. If they see a picture, people will be drawn to your poster. They will stop and read it. It could be a picture of a dog, if you're trying to get dog-walking jobs. Or it could be a teddy bear, if you are a babysitter.

▶

DON'T USE TOO MANY WORDS. But make sure to include:

- Your *name*

- Your **phone number or email address**

- The JOB you're looking for

Make sure your poster is easy to read. If you're using a computer to make your poster, choose a simple font. A swirly font looks good, but it won't help you get customers.

Be creative! Boring signs are no fun.

HANG POSTERS:

- at the grocery STORE

- on telephone *poles* in your neighborhood

- at the dog park

- at CHURCH

- on the bulletin board at SCHOOL

- at neighborhood *coffee shops*

- in the **elevator** of your apartment building

- at your parents' *workplaces*

▷ CHAPTER 3
THE BIG BUCKS:
Setting fees & saving smart

Everybody needs money. Even when you're a kid. You can definitely have fun *without* money. But if you want to buy a new shirt or go see a movie, you need to have your own money.

We've already talked about making money. But that's only half of it. If you're going to have money, you need to learn how to SAVE it. And you need to learn how to spend it — **wisely**.

Just remember: money isn't everything.

There will be some weeks or even months when you don't have as much money as you wish you did.

Maybe you're saving up for something, and you can't buy anything else in the meantime.

Maybe you haven't been making much money because it's been hard getting babysitting jobs.

Maybe you accidentally LOST your mom's favorite earrings, and you had to buy her new ones.

These things happen all the time. Grown-ups get bills that are *bigger* than they expected. Or they lose their jobs. Or they need a new car so they have to save money.

But since money isn't everything, you can still have lots of fun without money.

Look for free fun in . . .

- **YOUR TOWN:** The city where you live might have free events (like movies, museums, or festivals). Check newspapers, websites, and magazines.

- **YOUR SCHOOL:** There's always something going on at school, whether it's a sports activity or a potluck dinner sponsored by the PTA.

- **YOUR PARENTS:** Parents have a gift for being able to think of things you can do for fun, even when you're out of cash.

- **YOUR FRIENDS:** There's nothing better than just hanging out with friends, playing games, talking, and laughing. And that doesn't cost any money at all.

One of the things I like about being my own BOSS is that I get to choose how much to charge for my services. When you're a grown-up, your boss decides how much to pay you. But when you're a kid and you're your own boss, you can decide!

When I first started doing jobs for my neighbors, I thought I could just charge as much as I wanted. I told **Mr. Gomez** that I would help him with his lawn. But I said I would charge him $50 per hour. (I really wanted to buy tickets to the *Bad Dog* concert for me, Becca, and Monica. They cost $50 each. I thought if I worked for Mr. Gomez for three hours, I'd be able to afford three tickets.)

I was SHOCKED when Mr. Gomez said he couldn't afford to hire me at that cost. I decided I needed to earn whatever money I could, so I scaled back. I told him I would charge $10 per hour instead. He agreed, so after I worked for three hours, I made $30. (I decided to just buy my own ticket, and my friends bought their own tickets too.)

To figure out how much to charge, you have a few choices.

1. **DECIDE YOUR OWN PRICE.** (But be willing to make a deal, like I did with Mr. Gomez.) You can decide your price based on how much you have to spend on supplies, how hard the work is, and how much time you'll need.

2. **FIND OUT WHAT OTHER PEOPLE CHARGE FOR THE SAME SERVICE AND CHARGE THAT PRICE.** This is probably the easiest option, but it doesn't guarantee more customers.

3. **FIND OUT WHAT OTHERS CHARGE AND CHARGE LESS.** Jimmy found out that other lawn mowers charged $15 per lawn, per week. He decided that he'd rather have more jobs, so he charges $12 per lawn. Now his customers choose him over the more expensive people.

4. **DECIDE YOUR OWN PRICE AND REFUSE TO MAKE A DEAL.** (Not recommended!) Hey, maybe some people will pay you $50 per hour to help with their lawn . . . but I doubt it.

SAVING UP!

Saving money is really important, but it's not easy. It's a lot more fun to just spend your money as soon as you get it.

You usually don't get a lot of money at once. And you probably want things that cost a lot. So you'll need to *save up* to buy things like a new video game system or a bike or, in my case, a cell phone and a car.

I have a special place I keep the money I'm saving to buy a car. My dad helped me set up a savings account.

I also save up for other things. When I wanted to buy a new MP3 player, I started setting aside just a few dollars a week. If you save $5 every week, that's **$260** in a year. $10 a week is **$520!** It didn't take long before I had enough money to get the player I wanted.

If I save a little bit every week, I *barely* notice not spending that money. But I **DEFINITELY** notice when I have a lot saved up!

SAVINGS ACCOUNTS

Savings accounts aren't just a place to keep your money. You're actually LENDING money to a bank. They take your money and use it to give loans to other people. Then they pay you a little bit of money (usually about a penny or so per dollar per year) in return.

To get a savings account, just go to the bank of your choice and ask to open one. Some banks require an **adult** to be on the account for a kid. Some don't. It might be easiest for you to open a savings account wherever your parents have theirs.

Decide on a fixed amount that you will put into your savings account every week. It can be as little as one dollar or as much as everything you earn. It's up to you. But the more you deposit, the faster your account will grow. If you start depositing *one dollar* a week into your account at the age of thirteen, you'll have more than $350 by the time you're twenty, not including interest. But if you deposit **$5** every week, you'll have $1,820!

You have your CUSTOMER, your **JOB**, and your plan for taking care of your money. Now what? Now you **work**.

No matter how great your job is, it won't be all fun and games. Working is called "work" for a reason. But that's okay. Hopefully you've chosen work that you'll like. Then you'll have a **good time** while you're making some extra spending money. The more you like your job and the better you are at it, the more money you'll make.

Tips for succeeding at your job:

1. **BE PROMPT.** Always show up on time (or early). There's no excuse for being late to work. If you are going to be late, make sure to call to let your customer know.

2. **BE HONEST.** What if you accidentally break something? What if you lose something? What if the kid you're babysitting gets hurt? You need to tell your customer the truth.

3. BE FAST. Even if you're getting paid by the hour, you should try to do the job as quickly as possible. Your customer will appreciate it.

4. BE CAREFUL. Don't work so fast that you make mistakes. Your customer wants you to do your job right!

5. BE PROFESSIONAL. Wear appropriate clothes. Don't swear.

6. BE FRIENDLY. Smile and thank your customer, especially when he or she is paying you!

7. ADDRESS PROBLEMS. If your customer doesn't pay you on time, say something. If he or she wants you to work more than you agreed to work, say something. Speak up so that bigger problems don't happen.

Following these tips will build your reputation. More and more people will want your services. And you'll earn **more** and *more money*.

▷CHAPTER 4
A BUSY BALANCE:
You can't always do it all

The hardest part about work isn't working. It's fitting work in with the rest of your life.

If you're a busy thirteen-year-old like me, you have to **balance** work, friends, family, and school. Sometimes it feels like there's not enough time in the day for all of those things. So I've come up with some RULES that help me figure out what's most important.

1. Like my mom always says, **SCHOOL COMES FIRST.** No ifs, ands, or buts. School is my number-one job. I have to take it really seriously.

2. My *family* is second on the list. It's important to me to spend time at home.

3. My **FRIENDS** are next. My friends are the people who keep me from going crazy. They're there for me when I'm sad and when I'm happy. I need to be able to be there for them too.

4. Then comes **work**. It's important, but some other things are more important.

Work, fun, school, family. How can you keep it all organized? You need a *Claudia Calendar!*

Buy or make a calendar with big boxes. They should be big enough that you can write more than one thing on each day.

You'll also need a few different colored markers.

With a **BLUE** marker, go through your calendar and add important DATES. Think birthdays, holidays, the first day of school, vacations, etc.

Use an ORANGE marker to add your homework **ASSIGNMENTS** each day. (I bring my calendar to school and update my assignments after every class.)

Use a **GREEN** marker to write down babysitting jobs, lawn mowing days, or other jobs.

Use a **RED** marker for important TESTS.

With a PURPLE marker, add *fun things* you're looking forward to, like sleepovers and when certain movies come out.

UH-OH, I'M OVERBOOKED

It happens to *everyone*. You use the Claudia Calendar, but you forgot to write down plans to see a movie with your best friend on Friday. Then your favorite babysitting customer called and asked if you could babysit on Friday night. You said yes.

Friday comes. Your friend reminds you that you have plans that night. But you know you're scheduled to babysit, too.

So what do you do? You don't want to hurt your friend, and you did make those plans first. On the other hand, your babysitting customer is counting on you. It's too late for them to find another babysitter.

Friends should be a **HIGHER PRIORITY** than work. But in this situation, you should cancel plans with your friend. Hopefully she'll understand that you can't see the movie until Saturday night. (Offer to buy the popcorn to make up for it!) The job comes first because your customer is RELYING on you. You made an agreement, so now you are responsible for keeping your end of the deal.

Another situation: You're hanging out with your friends after school. Your dog-walking customer calls your house. She reminds you that you were scheduled to walk her dog an hour ago.

What do you do?

You have a few options.

1. Apologize and offer to come over right away to walk the dog. It might not work. (She might have already walked the dog.) But it's worth a try.

2. Apologize and offer a coupon for a free walk. You don't make money that way, but you prove that you're a professional who's sorry for making a mistake.

3. Don't apologize. Tell her you forgot. Then hang up and go back to chilling with your friends. **(HINT: This is never the right thing to do!)**

No matter what, **MAKE SURE YOU APOLOGIZE** to your customer. Remember, she might tell others about you. And you want whatever she says to be *GOOD!*

TRUE or FALSE

1. You get eight hours of sleep *every* night.

2. You have time for three good meals every day.

3. Your friends remember what you look like.

4. You've seen **at least** one member of your family in the past week.

5. You go to every single one of your classes.

6. Your grades are pretty good, and you're doing *all* of your homework.

7. Your dog (if you have one) has been walked and fed.

8. You have at least 30 minutes of free time every day.

9. You had time to brush your teeth last night and this morning.

10. You feel **HAPPY.**

If you answered FALSE to more than three of these statements, you are too **stressed!**

When you're too stressed, you need to cut back. Stress is really bad for you.

Here are just a few of the ways that stress can affect you.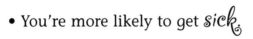

- You're more likely to get sick.

- Your scores on tests or homework might DROP.

- You might feel TIRED. But stress can also make it harder to fall asleep, which makes you more tired.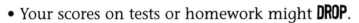

Get rid of stress by:

Watching a funny movie, playing your favorite video game, hanging out with your friends, playing sports, listening to music, taking **a bubble bath**, petting your dog or cat, hanging out with your family, RIDING YOUR BIKE, going for a walk, going shopping, or doing whatever makes you feel BEST!

School comes first. But sometimes it's hard to make time for school with all the other things going on in my **complicated** life.

If I don't do well at school, my parents won't let me do anything else! I won't be able to see my friends. And they *definitely* wouldn't be happy if my jobs were getting in the way of school.

So I need to make sure that school is my **NUMBER-ONE PRIORITY**. If I have a big test coming up, I need to make time to study. When I have an assignment due, I need time to do my homework.

I have a rule that every day, I figure out how much time I need to study or do homework. Then I add an hour to that, because sometimes I need more time than I think.

I like to get my homework done before I do anything else, but sometimes that's **impossible**. If I have a dog to walk at 3:20, I can't finish first.

When that happens, I don't make plans with friends for that day. I just save a little time to talk to them on the phone.

If I find myself *too tired* to do homework, I know I'm in big trouble. That means I've been taking on too much work or having too much fun.

I also have a hard time having fun when I know there's homework to do. It's hard to relax with your friends when you know you should be studying.

My advice is to finish your homework **AS SOON AS POSSIBLE** after you get home from school. Then it won't hang over your head. You'll feel free to do whatever you want, whenever you want. I even try to do this on Fridays. That way I have the rest of the weekend to have fun!

If you can't finish it right away, make sure to schedule time later that afternoon.

And if you can't finish it at all, you're doing too much other stuff. *Cut down* on working and hanging out with your friends. You need a schedule that lets you get your homework done.

McLean County Unit #5
201-EJHS

▷ CHAPTER 5
FOCUS ON FUN!
Make time to relax & recharge

You already know how to have fun. It's easy to have a good time with your friends. This section isn't about **having fun**. It's about *organizing fun*. Creating a club or planning a party are just two ways to organize some fun. And when you organize these sort of things, the planning is half the fun.

You can't force anyone to have fun. You can't promise that something will be fun. But you can set up a situation so that it'll be more likely to be fun.

Having fun is really important. It kind of **RECHARGES** your brain. If you're busy working and studying all the time, eventually your brain shuts down. It stays that way until you are able to relax a little. But if you have fun and work and study, it keeps your brain *nice and sharp*.

Look at it like this. Fun is the brain's way of letting off steam. It's a break from being busy all the time. It **STRENGTHENS** your imagination and makes you **happy**. That's why it's important to make time for fun.

Sometimes you'll be so busy between work and school that it seems almost IMPOSSIBLE to have any time left over for fun. That's not true. Having fun has to be a priority. You should always be able to find room for it.

So make sure to leave lots of room in your life for fun. Money isn't everything. Grades are really important, but they're not everything either. If all you're doing is studying, you're not going to be very happy.

Leave room for fun, and you'll be a much happier person!

Anna Dunlap is my school's popular princess. She started a club at the beginning of seventh grade. Everybody wanted to be in her club, the **GLORY GIRLS**. But Anna didn't let anyone into the Glory Girls unless they were popular, rich, or cheerleaders.

That left me, **Becca**, and *Monica* out, of course. We're just normal kids.

We pretended like we didn't want to be in Anna's club. But it actually hurt our feelings. All of the "**COOL**" girls were in Anna's club. We felt bad that we weren't cool enough to be included. Of course, none of us wanted to admit that. We finally told each other how hurt we were. And then something *great* happened. We decided to form our own club.

Our club is the *Whatever Club*. It isn't about being popular or perfect. It isn't about getting boys to like us or being mean to other girls. It's about having fun and doing whatever we want to do. (That's why we call it the Whatever Club!)

Here are some of the things the Whatever Club does:

- **SLEEPOVERS**

- **MAGAZINE DAY:** We each subscribe to different magazines. Once a month, we get together and read them all together.

- **PIZZA NIGHT**

- **SCRAPBOOK DAY:** We're making scrapbooks about middle school. Every two weeks we hang out in my tree house and work on our books.

- **SHOPPING**

- **NEW MUSIC MONDAY:** One Monday every month, we go to the mall and listen to music at the CD store.

- **CAMPOUTS** in the backyard

- **COOKIE BAKING**

- **BASEBALL GAMES:** We go to all of the **Harmon County Hawks** home games and to our friend Adam's games, too.

If you want to start your own club, you're in luck. It's pretty easy to do. The only thing you need is *friends* to start it with. The Whatever Club doesn't follow a lot of the structure that other clubs have. But that's **OKAY** — a club is whatever you want it to be!

Once you and your friends decide that you want to start a club, decide what your club's theme is. The theme of the Whatever Club is in its name. **It's whatever we want!** Our club is about having fun and hanging out together.

After you've picked a theme (or chosen to not have one) you should decide how often your club will meet. Ours meets **WHENEVER** we feel like it, but some clubs have set schedules.

For example, some clubs might meet the first Tuesday of every month. Others might get together once a month. It's up to you. You don't need to have a lot of structure if you don't want to.

Next, you might want to elect officers. *Officers can be:*

- **President** (runs the meeting): this person should be a great leader

- **Vice president** (runs the meeting if the president is gone): this person should also be a good leader

- **Secretary** (optional — if you want someone to take notes at club meetings): this person should be good with details

- **Treasurer** (optional — if your club will be collecting dues): this person should be trustworthy

Some clubs ask their members to each pay dues. That money goes toward things that the club pays for. For example, you might want matching T-shirts or to go on a club trip. The Whatever Club doesn't have dues. When we need to pay for something, we just all chip in.

I AM A T-SHIRT

Finally, you should decide on rules. The only rule of the Whatever Club is that we all have to agree. **WE'RE BEST FRIENDS, SO THAT'S NOT HARD AT ALL!**

▷ CHAPTER 6
LIFE OF THE PARTY:
How to throw the best bash

When most people think about things that are fun, one of the first things on their list is a PARTY!

I love parties. *Love them.* I love hanging out with lots of friends, eating good food, listening to good music.

I threw a pool party once that was SO FUN they wrote about it in our school paper. That's because I didn't just invite my friends. I wanted to have a huge bash, so I invited everyone in the seventh grade. Even *Anna Dunlap*.

I **EVEN** invited **Jenny Pinski**, our school bully. (I made sure that my uncle Diego was there to keep her from cannonballing into the pool and ruining everything.)

I'm not going to lie. It was a ton of work to put that party together. In fact, that's when I found a bunch of my odd jobs. I needed extra money because the pool and party room at the community center were *expensive*.

I had to work nonstop to come up with the money. I even *blew off* my friends. I forgot we had plans, and I was too busy to hang out with them.

They weren't happy about that. In fact, for a while I was afraid I wasn't going to have anyone to invite to the party.

But once I explained the situation to my friends, they all pitched in to help me.

Some of them helped me pay for the party room rental. Some of them helped by bringing food and drinks for the party. And some of them helped me set up for the party. My brother's band even played music at the party.

In the end, my party was a HUGE success. But it wouldn't have been if it wasn't for my friends.

I learned a lot from that experience. But the main thing I learned was that I'll never plan a party without my friends again! They helped make sure the party was a hit. Plus it was **a lot more fun** when they were involved with the planning. Make sure to involve your friends if you plan a party.

Want to have a party, but need a good excuse? Check out the next few pages for tips. I've included the Who, What, Where, When, and Why info you need to host the *perfect get-together*.

TIP: Be creative! You don't have to follow my ideas exactly. The most important part of a fun party is being with friends!

WHY: The reason for the party

WHERE: A good location for the party

WHEN: The perfect time for the party to happen

WHO: People who MUST be at the party. For me that's Monica, Becca, Adam, Tommy, and Peter

WHAT: Details you'll need to work out to have a great time

Birthday Party

WHY: Someone (you or a friend) is having a birthday!

WHERE: A pizza place

WHEN: The birthday night. This is a perfect party for a weeknight, since it happens at dinnertime. You'll have plenty of time to have fun before you have to go home and get ready for bed.

WHO: Close friends. (Everyone can pay for him or herself and chip in to pay for the birthday person's meal.)

WHAT: Pizza, soda, and cake. Laughing and having a good time. **FULL BELLIES AND LOTS OF FUN!** Make a reservation at the restaurant and order in advance if you can. If they don't have desserts, ask if you can bring a *birthday cake*. You can make one at home, or pick one up at the bakery or grocery store.

New Year's Eve

WHY: It's the end of one year and the beginning of the next.

WHERE: New Year's Eve can get busy, so it's best to have your **NYE BASH** at home. (That will make everyone's parents more likely to let them come to your party.)

WHEN: New Year's Eve, of course! Make sure to have your party last until after midnight so you can toast the new year.

WHO: For this type of party, it's nice to have your closest friends.

WHAT: Funny hats, noisemakers, and streamers for when the clock strikes twelve. Sparkling grape juice to toast with at midnight. Serve snacks like cheese and crackers, veggies and dip, and leftover holiday cookies. If the party starts after dinner, people will have eaten. If not, try serving make-your-own sandwiches or pizzas.

Other Holidays

WHY: It's time to *celebrate* a holiday! Halloween, Valentine's Day, St. Patrick's Day, or Talk Like a Pirate Day! There are tons of great holidays that deserve parties.

WHERE: For summertime holidays, outside is perfect. During the winter, you might want to stay inside, though! A fall holiday is the **perfect** excuse for a bonfire, and springtime holidays make great picnics.

WHEN: As close to the actual holiday as possible. Summertime parties are fun during the day, so that you can enjoy the sunshine. Winter parties can be coziest at night.

WHO: Close friends and good acquaintances. Holidays are a good time to invite everyone!

WHAT: Make the holiday the theme of your party. Heart-shaped cookies and hot cocoa for Valentine's Day. **CREEPY** decorations are perfect for Halloween. *Be creative!*

 Just for Fun

WHY: Everybody needs to have fun. If you're in need of some down time, a party is a perfect way to blow off some steam with your friends.

WHEN: A weekend night. That way you don't have to get up for school the next morning.

WHERE: Your house. The backyard makes a perfect location for **"just for fun"** parties. If it's too cold, a basement or rec room would work great too.

WHO: Whoever can come on short notice. This party is best planned fast!

WHAT: No need for decorations for this last-minute bash. For food, ask your friends to bring snacks. Frozen pizzas, cut-up veggies, and cookies from the cupboard will be tasty. Play music, watch DVDs, experiment with makeup and clothes. *Just have fun!*

Pool Party

WHY: It's **HOT** and you need to cool off. Or it's **COLD** and you wish it were summer. A pool party with your friends is a splashing good time.

WHEN: A Saturday afternoon is the perfect time to make waves.

WHERE: If you're lucky enough to have a pool, at your house. Otherwise, at any pool or beach you have access to.

WHO: Everyone you know. **THE MORE THE MERRIER!** You'll probably want to make sure some adults can come, too, since pools require adult supervision. (Bonus points if any of your friends are lifeguards!)

WHAT: Hot dogs and hamburgers are classic pool party food. Lemonade will help everyone cool off. Make sure there's plenty of good music. If you're outside, have sunscreen available. Indoors or out, have extra towels in case people forget!

▷ P.S.

Whether you're working or playing, it's **COMPLICATED** to be thirteen. I know that better than anyone else!

Luckily, being thirteen is also really fun. And it doesn't have to be as planned and organized as the things in this book. Fun happens all the time — not just when you plan it. I have lots of fun in between school, work, and homework. **And you should too.**

Even work can be fun. I love the dogs I take for walks. I even like babysitting. Since I don't have any younger brothers or sisters, it's a fun way to hang out with little kids.

The big thing I've learned about working is that if you're only doing it for the money, you're doing it for the wrong reason. The money should be the *icing on the cake*, not the only thing that makes you do your job.

I hope this book has helped you learn a little bit about more ways to *make your complicated life fun!*

A good job is:

1. One that you **LOOK FORWARD** to doing
2. One that makes you *feel good*
3. One that is near or with **people you like**
4. One that you would consider doing for FREE
5. One that leaves you with enough time for yourself
6. One that makes you **happy**
7. One that you choose to do because you *want* to do it
8. One that makes you feel better about yourself
9. One that *teaches* you something
10. One that HELPS you make money

ABOUT THE AUTHOR

Diana G. Gallagher lives in Florida with her husband and five dogs, four cats, and a CRANKY parrot. Her hobbies are gardening, garage sales, and grandchildren. She has been an English equitation instructor, a professional folk musician, and an artist. However, she had aspirations to be a professional writer at the age of twelve. She has written *dozens of books* for kids and young adults.

ABOUT THE ILLUSTRATOR

Brann Garvey lives in Minneapolis, Minnesota, with his wife, Keegan, their dog, Lola, and their very fat cat, Iggy. Brann graduated from Iowa State University with **A BACHELOR OF FINE ARTS DEGREE**. He later attended the Minneapolis College of Art and Design, where he studied illustration. In his free time, Brann enjoys being with his family and friends. *He brings his sketchbook everywhere he goes.*

GLOSSARY

acquaintances (uh-KWAYN-tuhns-iz)—people you do not know very well

allowance (uh-LOU-uhnss)—money regularly given to a child from a parent

biodegradable (BYE-oh-di-GRAY-duh-buhl)—something that breaks down naturally by bacteria

complicated (KOM-pli-kay-tid)—difficult to understand

environment (en-VYE-ruhn-mehnt)—the natural world of the land, sea, and air

organized (OR-guh-nized)—arranged in a neat order

priority (prye-OR-uh-tee)—something that is more important than other things

recommended (rek-uh-MEND-ed)—suggested as being good or helpful

reputation (rep-yoo-TAY-shuhn)—your worth as judged by others

responsibilities (ri-spon-suh-BIL-uh-teez)—duties or jobs

scheduled (SKEJ-oold)—planned

DISCUSSION QUESTIONS

1. Claudia is saving up for a car. *Are you saving up for anything?* How long do you think it will take you to reach your goal?

2. Of the jobs described, (babysitting, dog walking, lawn mowing, gardening, snow shoveling, running errands, and newspaper delivery) which is most **APPEALING** to you? **Why?**

3. If you started your own club, **WHAT KIND OF CLUB WOULD IT BE?** What would you name it?

WRITING ACTIVITY

Pretend you are an **ADVICE COLUMNIST** for your favorite
magazine. What advice would you give to solve these
problems?

1. I am throwing a PARTY for the end of the school
   year. I would like to invite my friends from band
   and my friends from basketball, but they don't
   know each other. Will it just be really *awkward*,
   or do you think we can all have fun together?

2. I have a snow shoveling business, and I have been
   really busy this winter. I forgot my homework
   last week, and now my parents say I have to quit
   shoveling. I *need* to make money, so what should
   I do?

3. I'm saving up for a digital camera. Every time I get
   about $50 saved up, I end up **BLOWING** it on a video
   game. **Help!** How can I be a better saver?

STRAIGHT FROM TEENS

Here's what real teens, just like you, have to say about dealing with work and play.

When you get a job, make sure you are going to enjoy it. Who wants to spend 30 hours a week doing something you don't enjoy?

—Kelli, 16

If you cannot stay focused in school and at home while having a job, then you may have to reconsider what's truly important. Above all, having a good home life and keeping up in school will benefit your future more than a job will.

—Tamara, 17

READ UP
FOR MORE GREAT ADVICE!

☆ *The Complete Idiot's Guide to Cool Jobs for Teens*
by Susan Ireland

☆ *For Girls Only: Wise Words, Good Advice*
by Carol Weston

☆ *Life Lists for Teens: Tips, Steps, Hints, and How-tos
for Growing Up, Getting Along, Learning, and Having
Fun* by Pamela Espeland

☆ *Teen Dream Jobs: How to Get the Job You Really
Want Now!* by Nora E. Coon

☆ *Too Stressed to Think? A Teen Guide to Staying
Sane When Life Makes You Crazy* by Annie Fox
and Ruth Kirschne

CLAUDIA

CRISTINA CORTEZ

MORE FUN with Claudia!

When you're thirteen, like Claudia, life is complicated. Luckily, Claudia has lots of ways to cope with family, friends, school, work, and play. And she's sharing her advice with you! Read all of Claudia's advice books and uncomplicate your life.